JAY COUNTY PUBLIC LIBRARY

1. Library materials are loaned for either 7 or 14 days and may be renewed once for the same period, so long as another patron has not requested that material.
2. A fine will be charged for each day kept overtime. No material will be issued to any person incurring such a fine until it has been paid.
3. Each borrower is responsible for all library materials drawn on his card and for all fines accuring on same.

THE SNOW STORM

*This classic short story
is presented without adaptation as part
of the Creative Classic series.*

THE SNOW STORM

ALEXANDER PUSHKIN

Illustrated by Mary Grandpré

Creative Education, Inc.
Mankato, Minnesota

Design: Tak Ming Wong
Editor: Ann Redpath
Biographical Sketch: Jim Dawson

Published by Creative Education, Inc.
123 South Broad Street, Mankato, Minnesota 56001.

LIBRARY OF CONGRESS
CATALOG CARD NO.: 82-74051

Pushkin, Alexander
   The Snow Storm.

   Mankato, MN: Creative Education
   40 p.

ISBN: 0-87191-923-0

To
the continuation of fine literature
for readers of all ages.

OWARDS THE END of the year 1811, a memorable period for us, the good Gavril Gavrilovitch was living on his domain of Nenaradova. He was celebrated throughout the district for his hospitality and kind-heartedness. The neighbors were constantly visiting him: some to eat and drink; some to play at five kopek "Boston" with his wife, Praskovia Petrovna; and some to look at their daughter, Maria Gavrilovna, a pale, slender girl of seventeen. She was considered a wealthy match, and many desired her for themselves or for their sons.

Maria Gavrilovna had been brought up on

French novels and consequently was in love. The object of her choice was a poor sub-lieutenant in the army, who was then on leave of absence in his village. It need scarcely be mentioned that the young man returned her passion with equal ardor, and that the parents of his beloved one, observing their mutual inclination, forbade their daughter to think of him, and received him worse than a discharged assessor.

Our lovers corresponded with one another and daily saw each other alone in the little pine wood or near the old chapel. There they exchanged vows of eternal love, lamented their cruel fate, and formed various plans. Corresponding and conversing in this way, they arrived quite naturally at the following conclusion:

If we cannot exist without each other, and the will of hard-hearted parents stands in the way of our happiness, why cannot we do without them?

Needless to mention that this happy idea originated in the mind of the young man, and that it was very congenial to the romantic imagination of Maria

Gavrilovna.

The winter came and put a stop to their meetings, but their correspondence became all the more active. Vladimir Nikolaievitch in every letter implored her to give herself to him, to get married secretly, to hide for some time, and then to throw themselves at the feet of their parents, who would, without any doubt be touched at last by the heroic constancy and unhappiness of the lovers, and would infallibly say to them: "Children, come to our arms!"

Maria Gavrilovna hesitated for a long time, and several plans for a flight were rejected. At last she consented: on the appointed day she was not to take supper, but was to retire to her room under the pretext of a headache. Her maid was in the plot; they were both to go into the garden by the back stairs, and behind the garden they would find ready a sledge, into which they were to get, and then drive straight to the church of Jadrino, a village about five miles from Nenaradova, where Vladimir would be waiting for them.

On the eve of the decisive day, Maria Gavrilovna did not sleep the whole night; she packed and tied up her linen and other articles of apparel, wrote a long letter to a sentimental young lady, a friend of hers, and another to her parents. She took leave of them in the most touching terms, urged the invincible strength of passion as an excuse for the step she was taking, and wound up with the assurance that she should consider it the happiest moment of her life, when she should be allowed to throw herself at the feet of her dear parents.

After having sealed both letters with a Toula seal, upon which were engraved two flaming hearts with a suitable inscription, she threw herself upon her bed just before daybreak, and dozed off: but even then she was constantly being awakened by terrible dreams. First, it seemed to her that at the very moment when she seated herself in the sledge, in order to go and get married, her father stopped her, dragged her into a dark bottomless abyss, down which she fell headlong with an indescribable sinking of the heart. Then she saw Vladimir lying on the grass, pale and bloodstained. With his dying breath he implored her, in a piercing voice, to make haste and marry him. . . . Other fantastic and senseless visions floated before her, one after another. At last she arose, paler than usual, and with an unfeigned headache. Her father and mother observed her uneasiness; their tender solicitude and incessant inquiries: "What is the matter with you, Masha? Are you ill, Masha?" cut her to the heart. She tried to reassure them and to appear cheerful, but in vain.

The evening came. The thought that this was the last day she would pass in the bosom of her family weighed upon her heart. She was more dead than alive. In secret she took leave of everybody, of all the objects that surrounded her.

Supper was served; her heart began to beat violently. In a trembling voice she declared that she did not want any supper, and then took leave of her father and mother. They kissed her and blessed her as usual, and she could hardly restrain herself from weeping.

On reaching her own room, she threw herself into a chair and burst into tears. Her maid urged her to be calm and to take courage. Everything was ready. In half an hour Masha would leave forever her parents' house, her room, and her peaceful girlish life. . . .

Out in the courtyard the snow was falling heavily; the wind howled, the shutters shook and rattled, and everything seemed to her to signal misfortune.

Soon all was quiet in the house: everyone was asleep. Masha wrapped herself in a shawl, put on a warm cloak, took her small box in her hand, and went down the back staircase. Her maid followed her with two bundles. They descended into the garden. The snowstorm had not subsided; the wind blew in their faces as if trying to stop the young criminal. With difficulty they reached the end of the garden. In the road a sledge awaited them. The horses, half-frozen with the cold, would not keep still; Vladimir's coachman was walking up and down in front of them, trying to restrain their impatience. He helped the young lady and her maid into the sledge, placed the box and the bundles in the vehicle, seized the reins, and the horses dashed off.

Masha wrapped herself in a shawl and went down the back staircase.
Her maid followed her with two bundles.

Having intrusted the young lady to the care of fate, and to the skill of Tereshka the coachman, we will return to our young lover.

Vladimir had spent the whole of the day in driving about. In the morning he paid a visit to the priest of Jadrino, and having come to an agreement with him after a great deal of difficulty, he then set out to seek for witnesses among the neighboring landowners. The first to whom he presented himself, a retired cornet of about forty years of age, and whose name was Dravin, consented with pleasure. The adventure, he declared, reminded him of his young days and his pranks in the Hussars. He persuaded Vladimir to stay to dinner with him, and assured him that he would have no difficulty in finding the other two witnesses. And indeed, immediately after dinner, appeared the surveyor Schmidt, with mustache and spurs, and the son of the captain of police, a lad of sixteen years of age, who had recently entered the Uhlans. They not only accepted Vladimir's proposal, but even vowed that they were ready to sacrifice their lives for him. Vladimir embraced them with rapture, and returned home to get everything ready.

It had been dark for some time. He dispatched his faithful Tereshka to Nenaradova with his sledge and with detailed instructions, and ordered for himself the small sledge with one horse, and set out alone, without any coachman, for Jadrino, where Maria Gavrilovna ought to arrive in about a couple of hours. He knew the road well, and the journey would only occupy about twenty minutes altogether.

But scarcely had Vladimir issued from the paddock into the open field, when the wind rose and such a snowstorm came on that he could see nothing. In one minute the road was completely hidden; all surrounding objects disappeared in a thick yellow fog, through which fell the white flakes of snow; earth and sky became confounded. Vladimir found himself in the middle of the field, and tried in vain to find the road again. His horse went on at random, and at every moment kept either stepping into a snowdrift or stumbling into a hole, so that the sledge was constantly being overturned. Vladimir endeavored not to lose the right direction. But it seemed to him that more than half an hour had already passed, and he had not yet reached the Jadrino wood. Another ten minutes elapsed—still no wood was to be seen. Vladimir drove across a field intersected by deep ditches. The snowstorm did not let up, the sky did not become any clearer. The horse began to grow tired, and the perspiration rolled from him in great drops, in spite of the fact that he was constantly being half buried in the snow.

At last Vladimir perceived that he was going in the wrong direction. He stopped, began to think, to recollect, and compare, and he felt convinced that he ought to have turned to the right. He turned to the right now. His horse could scarcely move forward. He had now been on the road for more than an hour. Jadrino could not be far off. But on and on he went, and still no end to the field—nothing but snowdrifts and ditches. The sledge was constantly being overturned, and as constantly being set right again. The time was passing; Vladimir began to grow seriously uneasy.

At last something dark appeared in the distance. Vladimir directed his course towards it. On drawing near, he perceived that it was a wood.

"Thank Heaven," he thought, "I am not far off now." He drove along by the edge of the wood, hoping by and by to fall upon the well known road or to pass round the wood; Jadrino was situated just behind it. He soon found the road, and plunged into the darkness of the wood, now denuded of leaves by the winter. The wind could not rage here; the road was smooth, the horse recovered courage, and Vladimir felt reassured.

But he drove on and on, and Jadrino was not to be seen; there was no end to the wood. Vladimir discovered with horror that he had entered an unknown forest. Despair took possession of him. He whipped the horse; the poor animal broke into a trot, but it soon slackened its pace, and in about a quarter of an hour it was scarcely able to drag one leg after the other, in spite of all the exertions of the unfortunate Vladimir.

Vladimir discovered with horror that he had entered an unknown forest.

Gradually the trees began to get sparser, and Vladimir emerged from the forest; but Jadrino was not to be seen. It must now have been midnight. Tears gushed from his eyes; he drove on at random. Meanwhile the storm had subsided, the clouds dispersed, and before him lay a level plain covered with a white, undulating carpet. The night was tolerably clear. He saw, not far off, a little village, consisting of four or five houses. Vladimir drove towards it. At the first cottage he jumped out of the sledge, ran to the window and began to knock. After a few minutes the wooden shutter was raised, and an old man thrust out his gray beard.

"What do you want?"

"Is Jadrino far from here?"

"Is Jadrino far from here?"

"Yes, yes! Is it far?"

"Not far; about ten miles."

At this reply, Vladimir grasped his hair and stood motionless, like a man condemned to death.

"Where do you come from?" continued the old man.

Vladimir had not the courage to answer the question.

"Listen, old man," said he, "can you find me horses to take me to Jadrino?"

"How should we have such things as horses?" replied the peasant.

"Can I obtain a guide? I will pay him whatever he asks."

"Wait," said the old man, closing the shutter. "I will send my son out to you; he will guide you."

Vladimir waited. But a minute had scarcely elapsed when he began knocking again. The shutter was raised, and the beard again reappeared.

"What do you want?"

"What about your son?"

"He'll be out presently; he is putting on his boots. Are you cold? Come in and warm yourself."

"Thank you; send your son out quickly."

The door creaked; a lad came out with a cudgel and went on in front, at one time pointing out the road, at another searching for it among the drifted snow.

"What is the time?" Vladimir asked him.

"It will soon be daylight," replied the young peasant. Vladimir spoke not another word.

The cocks were crowing, and it was already light when they reached Jadrino. The church was closed. Vladimir paid the guide and drove into the priest's courtyard. His sledge was not there. What news awaited him! . . .

But let us return to the worthy proprietors of Nenaradova, and see what is happening there.

Nothing.

The old people awoke and went into the parlor, Gavril Gavrilovitch in a night-cap, and flannel doublet, Praskovia Petrovna in a quilted dressing-gown. The tea-urn (samovar) was brought in, and Gavril Gavrilovitch sent a servant to ask Maria Gavrilovna how she was and how she had passed the night. The servant returned saying that the young lady had not slept very well, but that she felt better now, and that she would come down presently into the parlor. And indeed, the door opened and Maria

Gavrilovna entered the room and wished her father and mother good morning.

"How is your head, Masha?" asked Gavril Gavrilovitch.

"Better, papa," replied Masha.

"Very likely you inhaled the fumes from the charcoal yesterday," said Praskovia Petrovna.

"Very likely, mamma," replied Masha.

The day passed happily enough, but in the night Masha was taken ill. A doctor was sent for from the town. He arrived in the evening and found the sick girl delirious. A violent fever developed, and for two weeks the poor patient hovered on the brink of the grave.

Nobody in the house knew anything about her flight. The letters, written by her the evening before, had been burnt; and her maid, dreading the wrath of her master, had not whispered a word about it to anybody. The priest, the retired cornet, the mustached surveyor, and the little Uhlan were discreet, and not without reason. Tereshka, the coachman, never uttered one word too much about it, even when he was drunk. Thus the secret was kept by more than half a dozen conspirators.

But Maria Gavrilovna herself divulged her secret during her delirious ravings. But her words were so disconnected, that her mother, who never left her bedside, could only understand from them that her daughter was deeply in love with Vladimir Nikolaievitch, and that probably love was the cause of her illness. She consulted her husband and some of her neighbors, and at last it was unanimously decided that such was evidently Maria Gavrilovna's fate, that a woman cannot ride away from the man who is destined to be her husband, that poverty is not a crime, that one does not marry wealth, but a man, etc., etc. Moral proverbs are wonderfully useful in those cases where we can invent little in our own justification.

In the meantime the young lady began to recover. Vladimir had not been seen for a long time in the house of Gavril Gavrilovitch. He was afraid of the usual reception. It was resolved to send and announce to him an unexpected piece of good news:

the consent of Maria's parents to his marriage with their daughter. But what was the astonishment of the proprietor of Nenaradova, when, in reply to their invitation, they received from him a half in-sane letter. He informed them that he would never set foot in their house again, and begged them to forget an unhappy creature whose only hope was death. A few days afterwards they heard that Vladi-mir had joined the army again. This was in the year 1812.

For a long time they did not dare to announce this to Masha, who was now convalescent. She never mentioned the name of Vladimir. Some months afterwards, finding his name in the list of those who had distinguished themselves and been severely wounded at Borodino, she fainted away, and it was feared that she would have another attack of fever. But, thank Heaven, the fainting fit had no serious consequences.

Another misfortune fell upon her: Gavril Gavri-lovitch died, leaving her the heiress to all his prop-erty. But the inheritance did not console her; she shared sincerely the grief of poor Praskovia Petrovna, vowing that she would never leave her. They both left Nenaradova, the scene of so many sad recollections, and went to live on another estate.

Suitors crowded round the young and wealthy heiress, but she gave not the slightest hope to any of them. Her mother sometimes exhorted her to make a choice; but Maria Gavrilovna shook her head and became pensive. Vladimir no longer existed: he had died in Moscow on the eve of the entry of the French. His memory seemed to be held sacred by Masha; at least she treasured up everything that could remind her of him: books that he had once read, his drawings, his notes, and verses of poetry that he had copied out for her. The neighbors, hearing of all this, were astonished at her constancy, and awaited with curiosity the hero who should at last triumph over the melancholy fidelity of this virgin Artemisia.

Meanwhile the war had ended gloriously. Our

regiments returned from abroad, and the people went out to meet them. The bands played the conquering songs: "Vive Henri-Quatre," Tyrolese waltzes and airs from "Joconde." Officers who had set out for the war almost mere lads returned grown men, with martial air, and their breasts decorated with crosses. The soldiers chatted gaily among themselves, constantly mingling French and German words in their speech. Time never to be forgotten! Time of glory and enthusiasm! How throbbed the Russian heart at the word "Fatherland!" How sweet were the tears of meeting! With what unanimity did we unite feelings of national pride with love for the Czar! And for him—what a moment!

The women, the Russian women, were then incomparable. Their enthusiasm was truly intoxicating, when, welcoming the conquerors, they cried "Hurrah!"

"And threw their caps high in the air!"

What officer of that time does not confess that

to the Russian women he was indebted for his best and most precious reward?

At this brilliant period Maria Gavrilovna was living with her mother in a different province, and did not see how both capitals celebrated the return of the troops. But in the districts and villages the general enthusiasm was, if possible, even still greater. The appearance of an officer in those places was for him a veritable triumph, and the lover in a plain coat felt very ill at ease in his vicinity.

We have already said that, in spite of her cold-ness, Maria Gavrilovna was, as before, surrounded by suitors. But all had to retire into the background when the wounded Colonel Bourmin of the Hussars, with the Order of St. George in his buttonhole and with an "interesting pallor," as the young ladies of the neighborhood observed, appeared at the castle. He was about twenty-six years of age. He had ob-tained leave of absence to visit his estate, which was contiguous to that of Maria Gavrilovna. Maria be-stowed special attention upon him. In his presence her habitual pensiveness disappeared.

Bourmin was indeed a very charming young man. He possessed that spirit which is eminently pleasing to women: a spirit of decorum and observation, without any pretensions, and yet not without a slight tendency towards careless satire. His behavior towards Maria Gavrilovna was simple and frank, but whatever she said or did, his soul and eyes followed her. He seemed to be of a quiet and modest disposition, though report said that he had once been a terrible rake; but this did not injure him in the opinion of Maria Gavrilovna, who—like all young ladies in general—excused with pleasure follies that gave indication of boldness and ardor of temperament.

But more than everything else—more than his tenderness, more than his agreeable conversation, more than his interesting pallor, more than his arm in a sling—the silence of the young Hussar excited her curiosity and imagination. She could not but confess that he pleased her very much. Probably he, too, with his perception and experience, had already observed that she made a distinction between him and the others. How was it then that she had not yet seen him at her feet or heard his declaration? What restrained him? Was it timidity, inseparable from true love, or pride or the coquetry of a crafty wooer? It was an enigma to her. After long reflection, she came to the conclusion that timidity alone was the cause of it, and she resolved to encourage him by greater attention and, if circumstances should render it necessary, even by an exhibition of tenderness. She prepared a most unexpected dénouement, and waited with impatience for the moment of the romantic explanation. A secret, of whatever nature it may be, always presses heavily upon the human heart. Her stratagem had the desired success; at least Bourmin fell into such a reverie, and his black eyes rested with such fire upon her, that the decisive moment seemed close at hand. The neighbors spoke about the marriage as if it were a matter already decided upon, and good Praskovia Petrovna rejoiced that her daughter had at last found a lover worthy of her.

On one occasion the old lady was sitting alone in the parlor, amusing herself with a pack of cards, when Bourmin entered the room and immediately inquired for Maria Gavrilovna.

"She is in the garden," replied the old lady; "go out to her, and I will wait here for you."

Bourmin went, and the old lady made the sign of the cross and thought: "Perhaps the business will be settled to-day!"

Bourmin found Maria Gavrilovna near the pond, under a willow-tree, with a book in her hands, and in a white dress: a veritable heroine of romance. After the first few questions and observations, Maria Gavrilovna purposely allowed the conversation to drop, thereby increasing their mutual embarrassment, from which there was no possible way of escape except only by a sudden and decisive declaration.

And this is what happened: Bourmin, feeling the difficulty of his position, declared that he had long sought for an opportunity to open his heart to her, and requested a moment's attention. Maria Gavrilovna closed her book and cast down her eyes, as a sign of compliance with his request.

"I love you," said Bourmin. "I love you passionately. . . ."

Maria Gavrilovna blushed and lowered her head still more. "I have acted imprudently in accustoming myself to the sweet pleasure of seeing and hearing you daily. But it is now too late to resist my fate; the remembrance of you, your dear incomparable image, will henceforth be the torment and the consolation of my life, but there still remains a grave duty for me to perform—to reveal to you a terrible secret which will place between us an insurmountable barrier."

"That barrier has always existed," interrupted Maria Gavrilovna hastily. "I could never be your wife."

"I know," replied he calmly. "I know that you once loved, but death and three years of mourning. . . . Dear, kind Maria Gavrilovna, do not try to deprive me of my last consolation: the thought that you would have consented to make me happy, if. . ."

"Don't speak, for Heaven's sake, don't speak. You torture me."

"Yes, I know. I feel that you would have been mine, but I am the most miserable creature under the sun—I am already married!"

Maria Gavrilovna looked at him in astonishment.

"I am already married," continued Bourmin: "I have been married four years, and I do not know who is my wife, or where she is, or whether I shall ever see her again!"

"What do you say?" exclaimed Maria Gavrilovna. "How very strange! Continue: I will relate to you afterwards. . . . But continue, I beg of you."

"At the beginning of the year 1812," said Bourmin, "I was hastening to Vilna, where my regiment was stationed. Arriving late one evening at one of the post stations, I ordered the horses to be got ready as quickly as possible, when suddenly a terrible snow storm came on, and the post master and drivers advised me to wait till it had passed over. I followed their advice, but an unaccountable uneasiness took possession of me: it seemed as if someone were pushing me forward. Meanwhile the snowstorm did not

subside. I could endure it no longer, and again or-
dering out the horses, I started off in the midst of the
storm. The driver conceived the idea of following
the course of the river, which would shorten our
journey by three miles. The banks were covered
with snow; the driver drove past the place where we
should have come out upon the road, and so we
found ourselves in an unknown part of the country.
The storm did not cease; I saw a light in the distance, and I ordered the driver to proceed towards it.
We reached a village; in the wooden church there
was a light. The church was open. Outside the rail-
ings stood several sledges, and people were passing
in and out through the porch.

" 'This way! this way!' cried several voices.

"I ordered the driver to proceed.

" 'In the name of Heaven, where have you been
loitering?' said somebody to me. 'The bride has
fainted away; the priest does not know what to do,
and we were just getting ready to go back. Get out as
quickly as you can.'

"I got out of the sledge without saying a word

and went into the church, which was feebly lit up by two or three tapers. A young girl was sitting on a bench in a dark corner of the church; another girl was rubbing her temples.

" 'Thank God!' said the latter. 'You have come at last. You have almost killed the young lady.'

"The old priest advanced towards me, and said:

" 'Do you wish me to begin?'

" 'Begin, begin, father,' replied I absently.

"The young girl was raised up. She seemed to me not at all bad looking. . . . Impelled by an incomprehensible, unpardonable lightheadedness, I placed myself by her side in front of the pulpit; the priest hurried on; three men and a chambermaid supported the bride and only occupied themselves with her. We were married.

" 'Kiss each other!' said the witnesses to us.

"My wife turned her pale face towards me. I was about to kiss her, when she exclaimed: 'Oh! it is not he! It is not he!' and fell senseless.

"The witnesses gazed at me in alarm. I turned round and left the church without the least hindrance, flung myself into the sled and cried: 'Drive off!' "

"My God!" exclaimed Maria Gavrilovna. "And you do not know what became of your poor wife?"

"I do not know," replied Bourmin; "neither do I know the name of the village where I was married nor the post station where I set out from. At that time I attached so little importance to the wicked prank, that on leaving the church I fell asleep, and did not awake till the next morning after reaching the third station. The servant, who was then with me, died during the campaign, so that I have no hope of ever discovering the woman upon whom I played such a cruel joke, and who is now so cruelly avenged."

"My God! my God!" cried Maria Gavrilovna, seizing him by the hand. "Then it was you! And you do not recognize me?"

Bourmin turned pale—and threw himself at her feet.

Alexander Pushkin
1799 - 1837

38

ALEXANDER PUSHKIN, the greatest of all Russian poets, lived a tumultuous life that mixed poetry, politics, and love. His devotion to his wife and his strong sense of honor led to his death in 1837 when, at age 38, he was wounded in a duel.

During his life, Pushkin's writing dramatically changed all of Russian literature and, for the first time, exposed Russians to Western culture.

Pushkin was born in 1799 in Moscow to parents with very different backgrounds. His father was from an old, but poor, Russian noble family that had rebeled against Peter the Great. One of his relatives had been hanged by the Russian Czar. His mother was from a family that served Peter the Great and had become very wealthy.

Alexander knew about his conflicting heritage, and it influenced his writing. He was a poet of freedom and also a poet of Russian imperialism.

He learned about European poets by reading books in his father's vast library and, while still in school, began writing "romantic" poems similar to those written by French poets.

He also wrote political poems that got him into trouble with Alexander I, emperor of Russia. Alexander was sent into exile, where he was strongly influenced by the narrative poems of Lord Byron.

After fighting with a government official, Alexander was sent to a remote city and began writing about Russian customs and folkways.

A new czar, who liked Alexander's writing, came to power and Alexander was freed from his exile. But the new czar held great power over Alexander, and soon the poet began writing poems about how bad things were in Europe — which was a dramatic change from his earlier work.

In 1830 he married Nathalie Goncharov, a beautiful woman who was admired by the czar. Alexander and his wife spent much time in Moscow, and he soon owed a lot of money to the czar.

Seven years later a French royalist began courting Alexander's wife and the angry poet challenged him to a duel. Alexander was killed, and government officials, fearing a public uprising, carried his body at night to a monastery.